THIS • BOOK
IS • GIVEN
IN • HONOR • OF

Ross R. Reichenbach

on his Birthday,

May 30, 1993

·HARFORD DAY SCHOOL·

Space Spinners

Space Spinners

story and pictures by

Suse MacDonald

Dial Books for Young Readers New York

Published by Dial Books for Young Readers
A Division of Penguin Books USA Inc.
375 Hudson Street • New York, New York 10014

Copyright © 1991 by Suse MacDonald
Printed in Hong Kong
Typography by Amelia Lau Carling
First Edition
1 3 5 7 9 10 8 6 4 2

Library of Congress Cataloging in Publication Data
MacDonald, Suse. Space spinners / Suse MacDonald.
    p. cm.
Summary: Kate convinces her sister Arabelle to join her
in sneaking aboard the space shuttle so that they can be
the first spiders to spin a web in space.
ISBN 0-8037-1008-9 (trade).—ISBN 0-8037-1009-7 (library)
[1. Spiders—Fiction. 2. Space shuttles—Fiction.
3. Space flight—Fiction.] I. Title.
PZ7.M1525Sp 1991 [E]—dc20 90-23607 CIP AC

The full-color artwork was created by cutting shapes from
colored paper and applying them to a plain or hand-marbleized
background. It was then scanner-separated and reproduced
as red, blue, yellow, and black halftones.

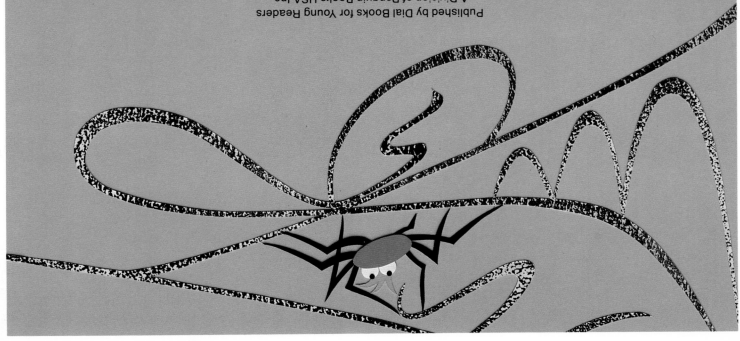

To Arthur who remembered it;
Sally and Stuart who helped shape it;
and Anita and Arabelle,
the NASA spiders who journeyed into space.

All the young spiders who lived in the supply closet at the NASA space center were practicing web making. Kate and Arabelle were almost done when their mother dropped by.

"Arabelle, your web is perfect and will be a great bug catcher." Arabelle blushed. "But Kate, as usual yours has too many large holes. Start again."

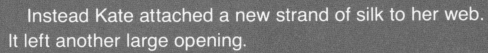
Instead Kate attached a new strand of silk to her web.
It left another large opening.

   "Kate," Arabelle whispered. "You are supposed to start
over."

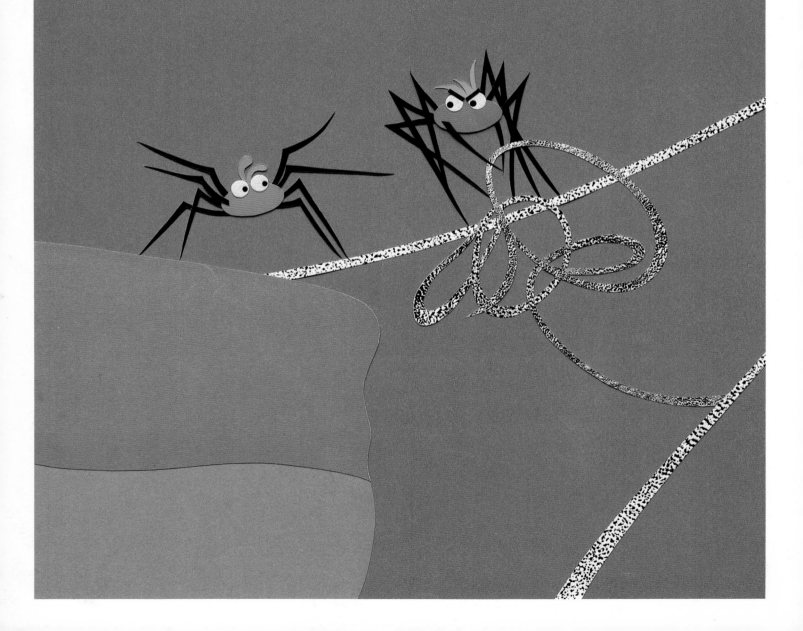

"Just spinning a perfect web is boring," grumbled Kate.
"I'd rather spin the first web in space."

"In space?" gasped Arabelle. "You can't do that."

"Sure I can. The shuttle leaves on Wednesday and I'm
going to sneak on board. Come with me."

"Oh no!" cried Arabelle. "It's too dangerous and Mother
would be furious!"

"Mother, Mother, Mother! You never do anything
exciting, Arabelle!" Kate said as she spun off.

"I do, too," said Arabelle. But she wondered if Kate was
right. And so, just to prove herself, Arabelle decided to go
along.

Early Wednesday morning the first astronaut came to get his helmet. He didn't notice the two spider sisters hitching a ride. Arabelle hid in his suit, while Kate rode boldly on his shoulder waving to the crowd.

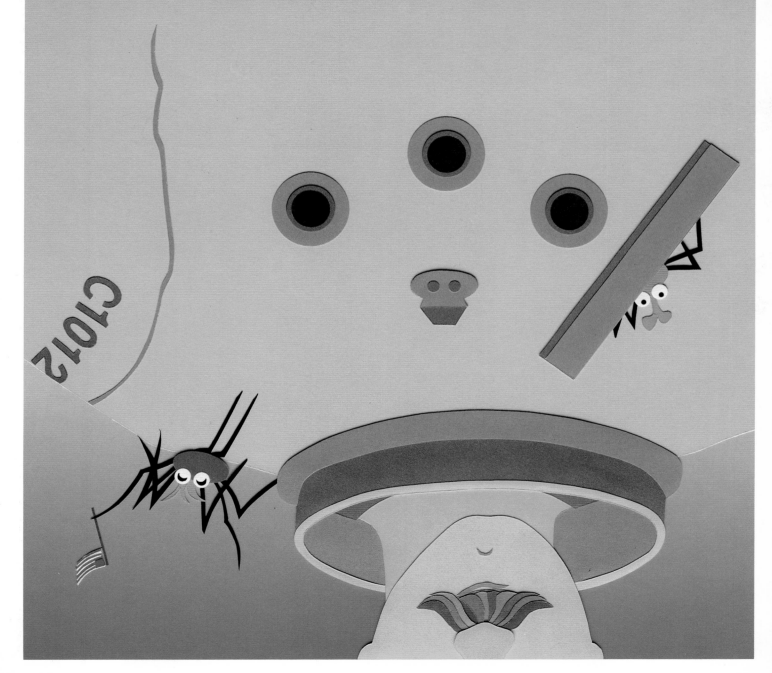

As soon as the door to the shuttle was firmly locked,
Arabelle scrambled into a spare helmet hanging near the
main viewing port and started spinning the tightest web
she had ever made.

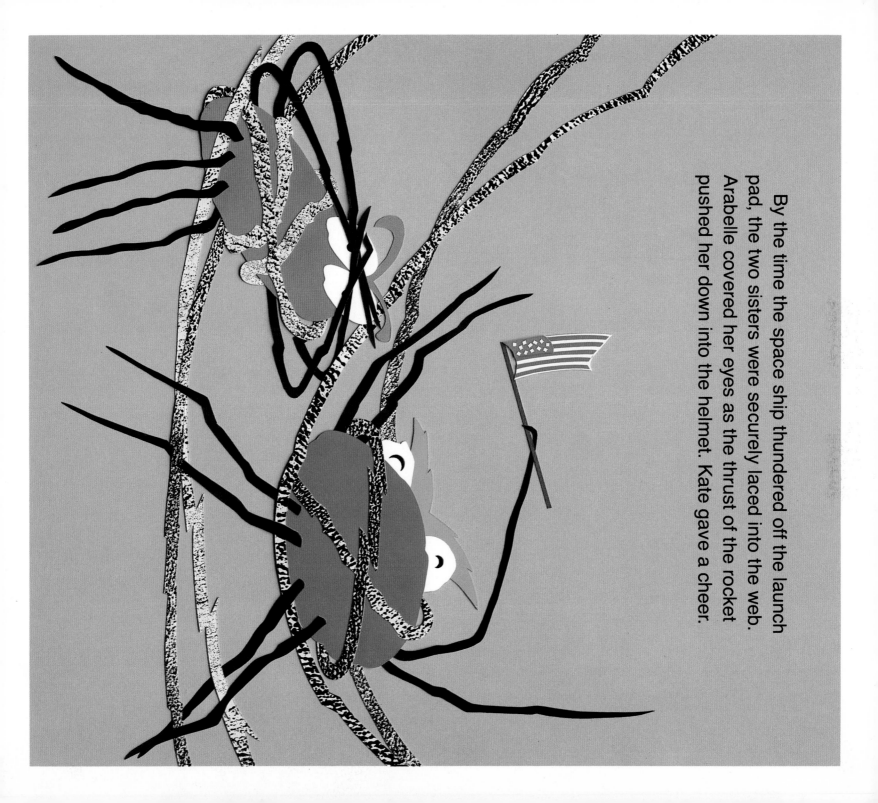

By the time the space ship thundered off the launch pad, the two sisters were securely laced into the web. Arabelle covered her eyes as the thrust of the rocket pushed her down into the helmet. Kate gave a cheer.

When it was quiet again, Kate freed herself and discovered gravity was not holding her down. "Look!" she said. "I can do somersaults in the air," and she crossed to the other side, being careful to avoid the opening in the helmet. If she floated out, how would she get back? Arabelle was too afraid to fly. Instead she counted the number of times the shuttle orbited the earth. Every ninety minutes the bright sun would set, and a dark and empty night enveloped the two sisters.

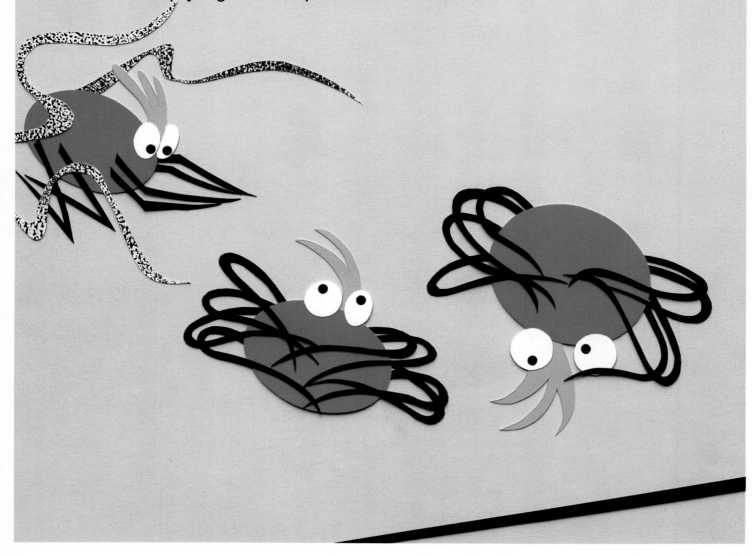

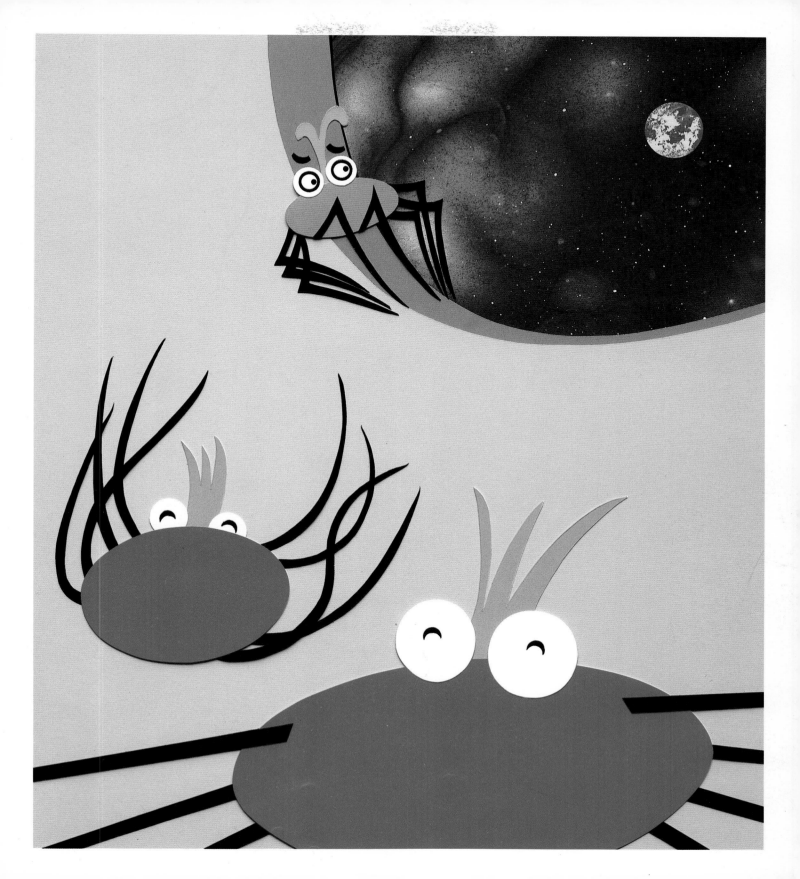

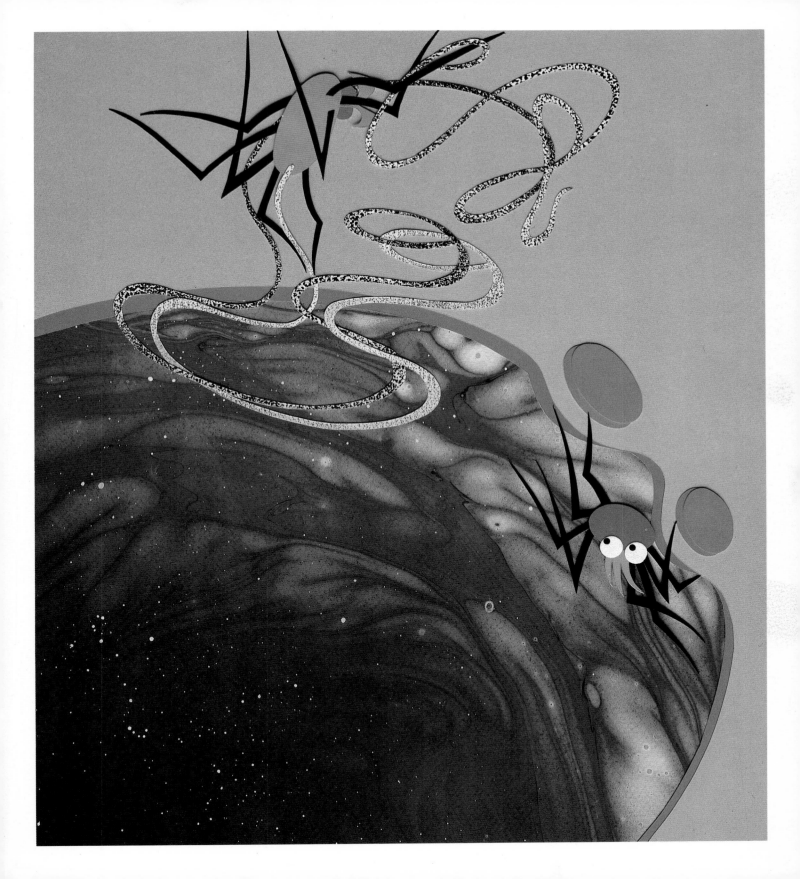

"Only twelve orbits to go," Arabelle said.
"We'd better start our web," Kate replied.
"Oh Kate, I'm too scared to spin here."
"Try, Arabelle. You're much better than I am."
Arabelle pulled out a strand of silk. But instead of rising
up on an air current, the strand landed on her head in a
sticky mass. As she struggled to free herself, she bumped
against the side of the helmet and drifted away.

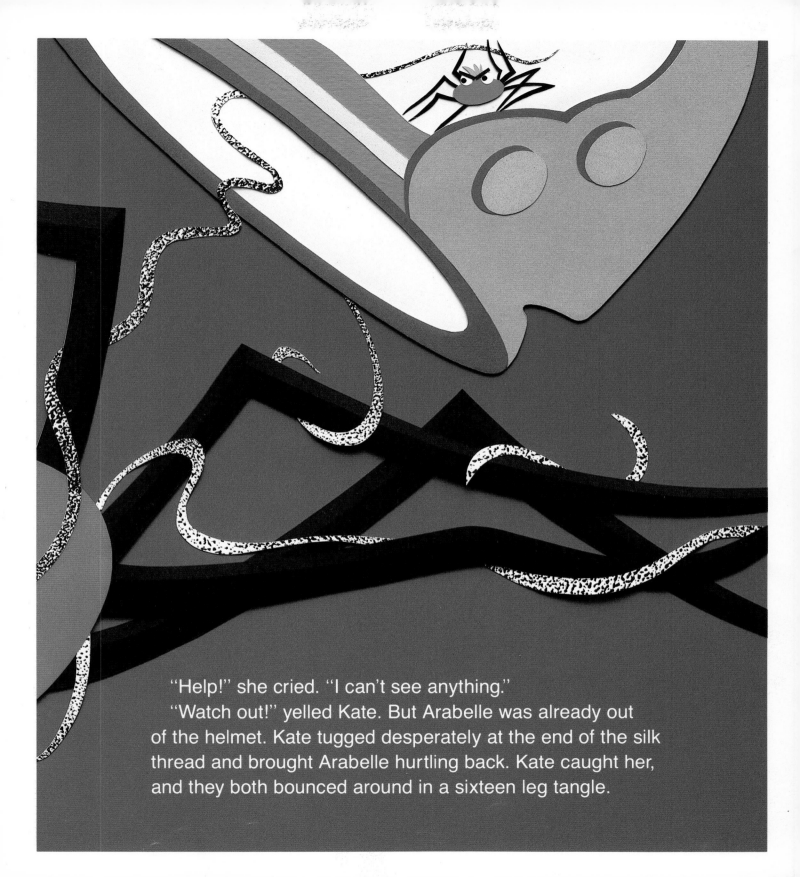

"Help!" she cried. "I can't see anything."

"Watch out!" yelled Kate. But Arabelle was already out of the helmet. Kate tugged desperately at the end of the silk thread and brought Arabelle hurtling back. Kate caught her, and they both bounced around in a sixteen leg tangle.

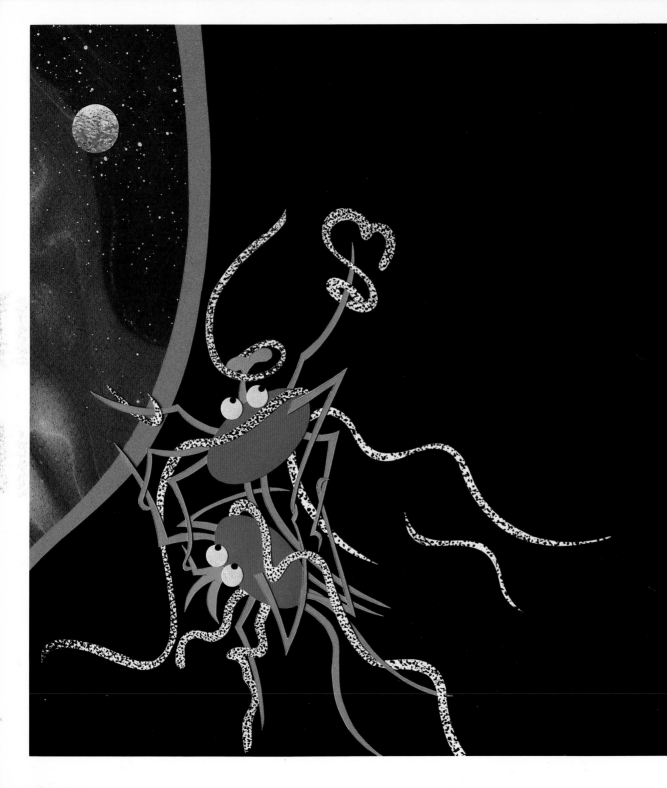

The two little spiders were suspended in darkness as the space ship passed out of the sunlight into the shadow of the earth.

"I wish I hadn't come," moaned Arabelle, clinging to her sister.

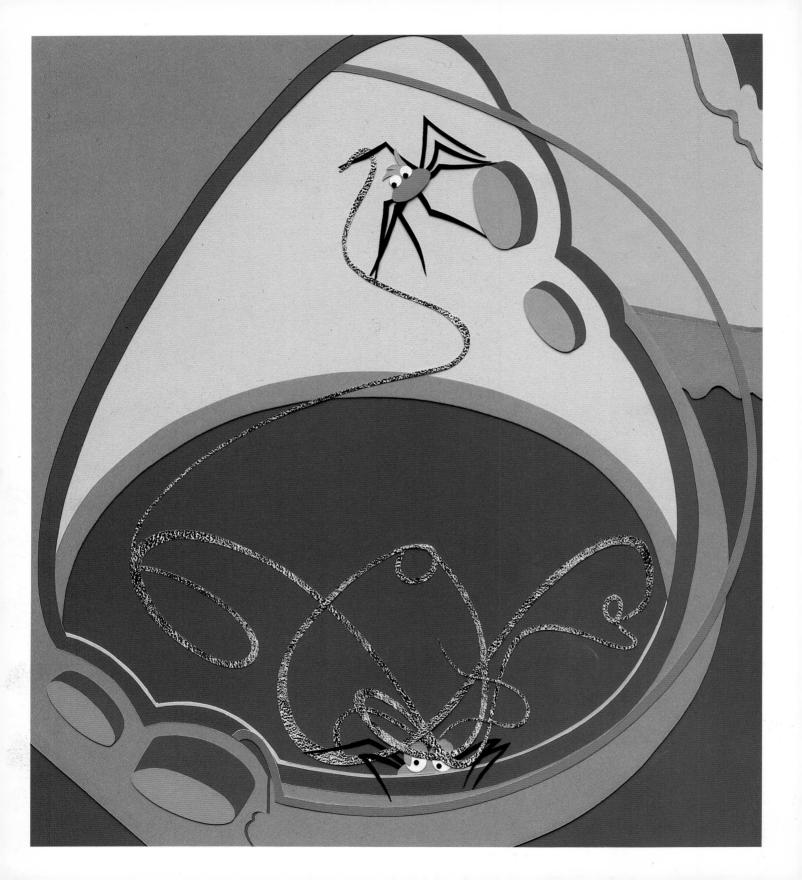

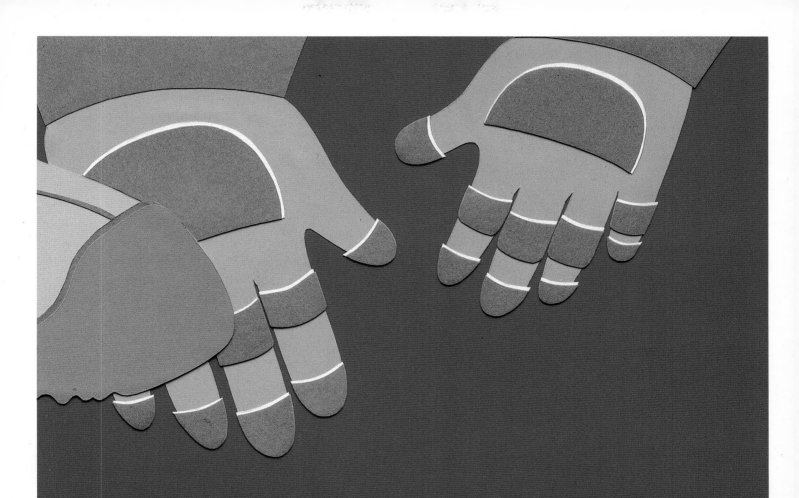

When the sun rose, Kate and Arabelle attached themselves to the side of the helmet.

"Arabelle, we've got to begin our web, we're running out of orbits. Quick, reel out some more silk and I'll carry it across." But Arabelle refused to let go of the helmet. So Kate reached above her sister and grabbed a strand of old silk. She floated to the other side of the helmet where she anchored the line.

"Hey Arabelle, look! Not bad for a first try. Now I'll try spinning myself."

Arabelle opened her eyes and watched Kate. "You're still not doing it right," she gasped. "The web is going to fall apart. There are no cross threads."

Without thinking, Arabelle hurried out along a thread and began stringing short pieces of her own silk between the long strands.

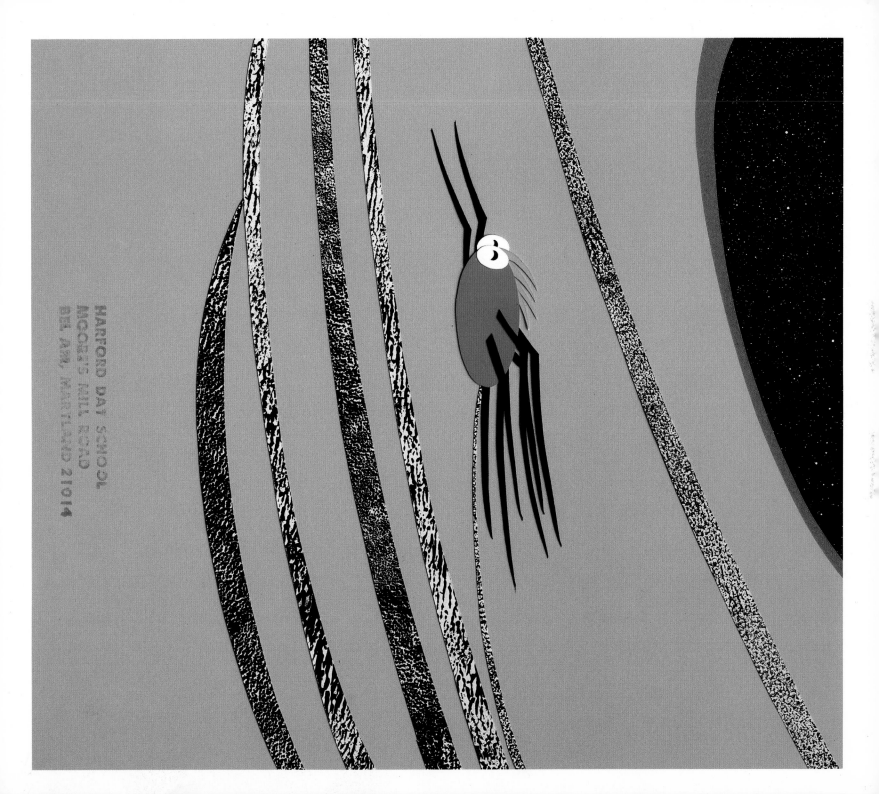

HARFORD DAY SCHOOL
MOORE'S MILL ROAD
BEL AIR, MARYLAND 21014

A few minutes later she looked over and saw that Kate was gleefully leaving wisps of silk hanging all over the place.

"Don't do that," Arabelle wailed. "It's messy!"

"Tack them down," said Kate. "I'm just trying to speed things up. There's only one orbit left."

The two sisters finished just as the sun rose once again from behind the earth. Their new web glistened.

"We did it, Arabelle. It's spectacular! The first web in space!"

"It is beautiful, Kate, but we'd better tie ourselves in. We're on our way home. I can't wait."

After the shuttle landed, Kate and Arabelle had a joyful reunion with their family and friends. Even their mother was too proud to be really angry with them for going.

Kate loved all the attention, and Arabelle grinned from leg to leg.